THE HEART OF TIME

Maliha Ayaz

THE HEART OF TIME

VIRGO
ebooks

Published by
Virgo eBooks Publishing
New York—Vermont
www.VirgoeBooks.com
office@virgoebooks.com

September 2015

Formatting: Constantin Dancu and Raul Folea
Cover design: Virgo eBooks

ISBN 13: 978-1-63041-767-3

Contents

This story was inspired by the following quote:

"Things done with negative intentions lead to more bad things, while things done with a pure heart always result in good things."

Sadaf Ayaz

Dedication

I dedicate this book to the following people:
To my parents, Ayaz Siddiqui and Shahnaz Siddiqi
who encouraged me, gave me advice,
and believed in me.
To my elder sister, Sadaf Ayaz,
who taught me that, if I could look for a light to turn on
when I couldn't think,
only then would I be able to write an actual book.
To my siblings, Huda, Marwa, and Zaid
whom I love and despise at the same time.

Where there is a will, there is a way. If there is a chance in a million that you can do something, anything, to keep what you want from ending, do it. Pry the door open or, if need be, wedge your foot in that door and keep it open.

Pauline Kael

Never give up, and be confident in what you do. There may be tough times, but the difficulties that you face will make you more determined to achieve your objectives and to win against all odds.

Marta Vieira da Silva

Prologue

"Sometimes, some people really get on my nerves," I said, my arms crossed, mouth twisted into a frown, as I faced the car window.

I could feel Mom smile as if she was really into this topic. She stopped at a red light and turned around, looking at me. "Oh, really? Like who?" she asked, playfully.

She turned to continue to drive as the green light appeared.

"Hmmm… Like Clara. She is such a showoff. She is always flaunting in front of me how both of her parents live with her and how I am a less perfect being because I do not have a dad who lives with me. It just frustrates me so much. I mean, it doesn't even make sense!" I said, turning to look at the back of her chair.

There was another red light. Mom turned to face me, and her eyes gleamed with sadness, anger and, at the same time, a memory. A mixture of emotions crossed her face as she let what I had said sink in. She closed her eyes, renewing in me the faint memory of something that had happened just two years ago but seemed much more distant. She frowned but said nothing. She remained ever so silent as we drove to Glory Home Middle School.

I looked out of the window, and my frown deepened as I saw a place of grief and mystery. It was an always-dreaded place—at least, for me.

SHADOWFLEET GRAVEYARD said the sign in large letters.

Death is scary, I thought to myself.

Shadowfleet Graveyard was pretty scary as well.

Its dark, frightening shadows seemed to reach out to me through the window of my car. It was as if someone was watching me, looking at my every move, every twitch of my muscle, every beat of my heart, every breath I took, and every word that escaped my mouth.

It was always gloomy and dark there. Even when the sun was shining its brightest and perkiest, it was still a dim and lonely place.

Its bare trees looked over the dead as if making sure they stayed there. They seemed to be protecting the living from the dead—as if expecting that, one day, the dead would try to take over the bodies of the living. I shivered and brushed that thought away. My greatest fear was cemeteries.

Our town had a legend that told of strange things happening at Shadowfleet Graveyard. Once, when I was a little girl, I heard that another girl—I think her name was Elizabeth Parker—walked by the graveyard at night. When she passed it, the gates creaked open as if moved by an invisible force. That force took over the little girl's body, and she entered the graveyard without knowing what she was doing. Apparently, she ended up running to the end of the cemetery and falling into a deep hole of dark magic. She died, making the graveyard's name ring even truer. Ever since I heard that legend, I had gotten goosebumps every time I went near the cemetery, or even when someone talked about graveyards or the dead. But no other graveyard gave me chills like this one did.

Bella once told me that sometimes loud, piercing noises shot through the sky, seeming to come from the Shadowfleet Graveyard, even though no one was there— that is, no one alive...

I had also heard that sometimes a hand, or something else—something like a vine or a moving plant— would emerge from the ground to grasp the foot of anyone it could, holding on so tightly that that person could not escape. Then, it would pull them down into a hole!

What happened to the person afterward was something that no one knew—and probably, no one would ever know, unless someone who was taken from the vine came back alive. But everyone knew that anyone who set foot on the deep-rooted, filthy dirt of the graveyard would never be heard from again. The situation has worsened so much that no one buries anyone in there anymore. And the people who were buried, their loved ones only come to pay their respects from afar.

I shuddered at these creepy stories. Everyone in town believes in the stories, so naturally, the fear is instilled in me.

Did I not tell myself to stop talking about it? Ughhh! I thought.

"Amber?" Mom said, interrupting my not-so-important thoughts.

"Yes, Mom?" I replied.

She seemed to have figured out what to tell me about my problem at school.

I stared into her trusting eyes as she said, "You will always find people who give you trouble in life, but never, ever give up. You are a ray of sunshine, my dear. Shine on whatever you can, and shine as long as the sun is up." I smiled at her words. Leave it to my mom to make me optimistic while I was at my most pessimistic.

"And you are my ray of sunshine," I said with a big, gentle smile, reaching over to kiss my mom on her cheek. "I promise to never, ever give up and to be strong whenever I have to."

"That's the Amber I know," Mom said with an even bigger smile. "I love you."

"I love you too, Mom," I replied with a smile plastered on my face.

"Be strong, my love," she said. Those were her last words.

And
then
it
happened.

No matter how prepared you think you are for the death of a loved one, it still comes as a shock, and it still hurts very deeply.

Billy Graham

Chapter ONE

I gasped as I awoke.

I was breathing heavily. I briskly moved the hair from my face.

"Quick!" someone said.

"She's awake," said someone else, sounding relieved.

"…Getting off the anesthesia," said another voice.

Beep bip bip beep!

The police car's noise just would not stop.

"I love you," I heard someone say in Mom's voice.

I shut my eyes tight.

"Stay with me, baby," someone said.

"I'm with you, Mom. Momma?" I whispered.

"Momma!" I cried. "I'm with you, I'm with you, Mom!"

My eyes fluttered open once again. I was dizzy.

What happened? I thought to myself.

Someone reached out to hold my left hand and shook it vigorously as if he had never met me before. I suddenly realized it was my dad's hand.

I blinked a few times. There were wires made of I-have-no-idea-what almost everywhere on my body.

Wait, what? Dad?

What happened? Why is Dad here? He had not been here for a few months. He was not supposed to come for another two months, until his twice-annual visit. Ever since my parents got divorced, my dad, James William, had lived in Philadelphia and only came to visit once every six months. That was when my mom, Megan William, was not around.

Dad's usual warm, brown eyes held both worry and something else as he stared into my blue eyes.

Fear.

That's what I saw in his eyes.

Tearing, heartbreaking fear.

I looked away. It was too painful to see Dad like this, especially since I had not seen him for a while. The first look I saw on his face was one of fear, and it scared me.

I was surprised by the number of people in the room. When I turned to look at them, my heart went wild with the idea that something was indeed wrong. Everyone was staring at me with pity. There were doctors and nurses with uniforms on and defeated faces, looking at me like they felt sorry for me.

"What's going on?" I asked.

But everyone was silent.

As if I wasn't normal or something.

As if I had become abnormal.

What on Earth was going on? Moreover, why was I being ignored?

A group of people surrounded the hospital bed. Some visitors and family members were also there.

"Why won't anyone tell me anything?" I yelled. A few of them moved away from a bed on the other side of the room when they heard my outburst.

Others had just put down parchments, gifts, cards, and flowers on my bedside table.

Just then, Dad spoke and broke the silence, which had seemed like it would never end. Gulping, he said, "Amber, honey? Everything will be alright, darling. Just hang on." Tears welled in my eyes. What was going on? "Do not cry, baby, I am here. Daddy is here for you.

Everything will be okay," Dad said, tightening his grip on my hand.

I didn't reply. I just stared at the wall.

And then out of nowhere, I realized that Mom wasn't there. I searched the eyes of the people around me one more time to make sure I wasn't missing her. But not a single pair of eyes matched the blue hue that only my mom's had. I gulped. Mom would never, ever leave me.

Never, ever.

"Where is Mom?" I screeched. Pin-drop silence enveloped the room as all the adults looked at each other. Their eyes voiced the concern in their thoughts.

"Dear," said a doctor with a British accent as he weaved through the nurses to the side of the bed. He exchanged a look with Dad before taking my hand in his. "My name is Dr. Vanderbeek. I am very sorry to inform you that your Mom is in critical condition after the car accident."

Car accident?!

Is that what happened? Is that why I am here?

"You are out of danger, but I am afraid I cannot say the same for your Mom. Just pray for her, dear. That is the best you can do," Dr. Vanderbeek said.

I gulped and looked over at the bed on the other side of the room.

For a second, I was confused until it clicked. Then I smiled in relief.

"You're joking, aren't you? You're trying to trick me! It's a prank, isn't it?" I said, laughing. A few of the people turned away, and some even left the room, tears swimming down their cheeks. "See? I knew it! It was all a lie! I should have known! Well done, Dad, you really pulled off this one. You got all these people and even an appointment at the hospital for a prank. Gosh, Dad, I should have known. You are the best!" I looked at Dad, but his face held pity and grief, and his eyes were closed. The air told me something wasn't good. My voice dropped to a low whisper as my heart clenched. I silently prayed to God: Please make everything okay, God. Please.

"It's a prank... right? Right, Dad?" I asked once again when I still didn't get a reply.

Dad's face became red, and a few tears dripped down his nose. A few nurses patted his back with heartbroken eyes. He stared at me, ashen, shook his head in grief and misfortune, and mouthed, no. He looked down on the floor in pain as a puddle of tears began to form there.

I shook my head vigorously. "No! It cannot be! She cannot di..." I started yelling and then stopped at the last word. I could not say it. I couldn't utter the word. The image of Mom in a coffin with bugs, gone from my life, without her lovely smile, her beautiful blue eyes—I just could not take it.

After a while, the room began to clear out. Soon, everyone was gone except my dad and me. I asked him once again: "Where is she?"

Dad was completely silent as his big, comforting hands held mine, and my thoughts swam through my head in a hurry.

Then, Dr. Vanderbeek came in, eyes full of grief, and said, "Mr. William, I need to speak with you privately." Dad and the doctor went outside. After a few minutes, Dad came back in, wide-eyed. Tears streamed down his cheeks again, but this time even harder. He grabbed a few tissues from a box on the table and sat down, weeping. My mouth went agape at his sudden outburst.

I jumped out of the bed, ran to my dad, and sat down next to him, taking the tissue box with me. He grabbed a few more tissues, then continued to cry his heart out. I patted his back and murmured a few comforting words. I had no idea why he was crying so hard. But I knew if that I were crying like this, Dad would be there, doing the same thing that I was now doing for him.

He started to hiccup between tears. I held him in an embrace as his sobs lessened. Then I waited for him to explain why he was crying so hard.

When he began to simply stare off into space and hiccup, I realized he wouldn't tell me unless I kept asking. So I did. "What happened?"

Dad wiped his eyes and didn't say anything. The doctor came back inside, and I asked immediately, "What happened? Why is he crying?"

The determination in my eyes must have gotten to the doctor because, like a robot, he immediately answered, "Your mom's condition was worse than we thought. I'm sorry to inform you that she passed away a few minutes ago."

I didn't process the words at first. But then, I realized what he had said and collapsed back into the chair, my mouth slightly opened in surprise—then I cried like a lunatic. I grabbed tissues from the box. I soon felt hands rubbing my back. "It's okay," I heard the doctor say softly. Then, I felt my dad's hand wiping my face. We had a good cry together. Finally, when we were both done, I said in a hoarse voice, "I can't believe it."

Dad hugged me.

He looked at me straight in the eye and nodded. "It will be okay. She is here. She is… She is in here…" He put his hand where my heart was. He looked into my teary blue eyes. "She is up there," he added, pointing toward the ceiling. His face got redder and redder. "She is… She is gone." He broke into tears. "She will… She will always… always be with us," he said.

It's just a nightmare. It's just a nightmare. It isn't real, I tried to convince myself.

I will shut my eyes, and when I open them again, I will not be in the hospital anymore. I shut my eyes ever so tightly and kept them closed for such a long time that I was afraid I had fallen asleep…

I opened my eyes.

I was not in a hospital.

Dad was not with me.

Mom was not with me either.

There was no one around me.

There was only silence, and there always would be.

There are only two mistakes one can make along the road to truth; not going all the way, and not starting.

Buddha

Chapter TWO

It had been over two weeks since we buried Mom. Even though Dad had gotten a transfer and now worked at the Manhattan branch of his company, I had asked him if I could stay with Bella at her house. He was a bit hesitant, but he understood why.

For him, dealing with the pain was about facing it head on. He felt better when Mom's things surrounded him. I, however, broke down at each reminder of her. Every time Bella's mom would sing "Twinkle, Twinkle Little Star," I remembered when I was little, and Mom sang it to me. Immediately I would lose hold of myself, my legs would feel wobbly, and I would almost faint. But then I would remember what Mom told me.

"You are a ray of sunshine, my dear. Shine on whatever you can, and shine as long as the sun is up." I heard Mom's words once again, and after that reminder, I couldn't help but start thinking:

What was a child without his or her mother?

What was I without my mom?

As the days passed, and I felt more and more hopeless, the answer was clear: Nothing.

Thank God, Bella realized this and talked to her mom about it. I do not think God could have granted me a better friend than Bella Richard. She was the biggest blessing I had at the moment.

She tried her very best to make sure I did not go down the drain and get clogged. She kept me company to the best of her abilities, making sure I was happy or, at least, sane. She brought me food for every meal. When I wouldn't eat it, she quietly fed me, making sure that I stayed healthy.

Though she was my age, she was taking care of me like I was her daughter. That was probably the reason why I let her get away with doing those motherly things. I really missed my mom, and it was nice to feel like I still had one, even though Bella was just my best friend.

Maybe it was because of her eyes that I always felt at home. I couldn't help it. She had blue eyes, the color and shade of those I wanted to see.

I would never, ever tell her that her blue eyes reminded me of my mom. I was too scared that I would break down into never-ending sobs and even more afraid I wouldn't cry—that I would just give up. I would never, ever tell Bella that, when she hugged me, I weirdly felt like I was in the arms of my mom. She held me with the same amount of affection as my parents. But I thanked her every day. Her eyes were a reminder of Mom, but more so, they were a reminder of care and trust. I could not refuse Bella, ever.

One day, I was sitting on the window sill in her room. Bella's family, like mine, owned a pretty nice house. Although most of the bedrooms were on the second floor, Bella occupied the attic, and the window right at the tip of the attic had a nice sitting place. The window overlooked a peaceful flower garden, and it brought some tranquility and smoothness to my mind. The flowers reminded me of the happy days I had spent helping my mom plant flowers all around our backyard. It made my eyes burn to think about, but I suppressed the tears.

Bella took a seat next to me. "Hey!" she said. Immediately, she plastered a bright, positive smile on her face.

"Hey," I said with a curt smile. "How was school?" I asked. I had not been going to school since Mom died, partly because it felt weird to go without her help and partly because I wasn't feeling well from the accident. Thank God the adults did not insist on me going.

"It was okay. Obviously it was boring without you, so it was a pretty big drag," Bella said as she smiled again. "You should start school again, Amber. I feel like I am in prison without you there."

I looked back at the garden and hid my smile. I said, "I will start again. I promise. I just need a little more time. So, what did you do today?" I asked to distract her again.

"Nothing, really, just screamed a lot at Clara for being so mean and annoying. Ha-ha. She's not that bad, you know. She was telling me how she felt terrible about what happened to your mom, and she wishes she had never said those mean things to you. She said she wanted to come over and apologize. I told her she can come, but not now. You're still settling in. Is that okay?" Bella asked, worried that she had said the wrong thing.

"Yeah, of course," I said appreciatively. She was already doing so much, and she was still worrying. I don't think anyone could've had a better best friend. "I don't want to see any more people either. I mean, it's nice to see that people care, but every time someone talks to me, it reminds of the pain again. Then all I want to do is run to Mom's bed and sleep with her smell around me," I replied.

"I know, Amber. I can understand. I can't imagine how I would feel if my mom died in an accident." Bella said as she hugged me tightly. I held on to her. She was the only one holding me up right now, and I really needed her.

"Thanks for everything," I said.

Bella sighed. "I got the memo the last 54 times you said that." We laughed.

"Sorry," I said. "It's just that you have helped me so much. I don't think I can ever stop thanking you."

"I understand," she paused, nodding and placing a hand on my shoulder. Then she exclaimed, eyes brightening, "Oh, look what I got yesterday!" She held up the necklace that she was wearing.

"I was going to tell you yesterday, but you were sleeping, so I decided to save it for today's special gossip topic," she said with an excited giggle, wiggling her fingers in a mysterious way as she moved closer to show me the necklace. She would not take it off, and I could understand why. The necklace was a masterpiece of jewelry. A beautiful, crystal-clear circular gem hung on a silver string of steel. The center of the crystal had intricate designs like you would typically find in a watch. The edges of the gem were designed with sharp lines that looked like skulls and swords. I was mesmerized. It was so beautiful and elegant—in a creepy way.

Bella had given me the best distraction ever. Bella and I loved playing dress up; clothes, jewelry, and makeup were our favorite things in the world.

"Oh my God! It's so pretty! Where did you get it from?" I asked excitedly as I held it and looked at it in awe. I couldn't take my eyes off of it. "I mean, you must have bought it. No one would just leave something as valuable as this lying around."

"Okay, so… I need a favor," Bella said. "Please do not tell Mom any of this. I kind of told her I just found the necklace on the ground, but that's not exactly true. I am positive that she would get very mad if I told her the truth or if she found out the truth. So please don't mention this to her." My mouth went agape. Bella never lied to her mom.

"You shouldn't hide stuff from your mom, Bella… You never lie to your mom," I said, astonished that she was doing this. It wasn't like her ever to say or do anything other than what she was supposed to.

"I know, I know, but still, I felt like I had to this time. Do you see how beautiful this is?" Bella said as she raised the necklace and brought it closer to my face. "Mom would never let me keep it."

"I know… but still," I said, looking into her excited eyes.

"But still, nothing. Do you want to know the story or not?" Bella asked, raising an eyebrow. I sighed.

"I do, I do. Tell me the real story. I will not tell your mom, do not worry. It isn't my story to tell anyway. You know me, I am not a fan of tattle tales, so I am not one," I said, wrapping my pinky around hers.

"Okay, so I was walking home from our school yesterday, and… you know how I always walk through Shadowfleet Graveyard to get home?" Bella said.

"Yeah," I said, nodding vigorously. That was why I hated walking home with Bella. She found the creepiness of that place beautiful. She wasn't scared of death; she loved the idea of it. She was weird.

"Well, when I was walking, right at the corner of the entrance, I saw something really shiny. It was so bright, Amber, I'm sure you can't even imagine it!" Bella cried out. She was so excited. "Anyway, even though the necklace was near Shadowfleet Graveyard, I was really curious, so I walked over and picked it up. While I was picking it up, some old lady came up behind me. I think she had been walking around, but I had not noticed her. She started telling me some weird things, such as that it was 'our' time and that this necklace would 'save' me. She said that this necklace would be 'our' savior or whatever. I do not know who 'our' is—like, me and who else? Anyway, she told me I was the chosen one, and then she walked over and took the necklace from my hand. And—" She had more to say, but I couldn't help but cut her off.

"Hold on. No offense, but that is incredibly creepy. And all of this happened in front of Shadowfleet Grave-yard? The scariest graveyard in, like, the world," I said, pushing a hand through my hair.

"Yeah," Bella replied.

"That is so... omen-ish," I continued, trying to explain to her how strange I found the whole situation to be.

"Omeneh-what?" Bella asked, not understanding the meaning of the word.

"Omen. You know, like it kind of foreshadows something bad that is going to happen," I said. I was surprised that she didn't know the word. Bella and I read books together all the time when we were free, so we usually had the best vocabularies in our school.

Bella laughed at me, however. "Amber, listen, you have not even heard the whole thing yet. Pay attention, and stop getting distracted!" she said, pushing me playfully. She was so excited and amused by her story that she couldn't contain herself. Bella was always a patient person and, for the first time, she was acting impatient. So I let her have her moment.

But, from what it looked like so far, I was not exactly sure that I should let her have it. It still felt like stealing, somehow, though it was merely a gift from a peculiar old woman. I mean, doesn't that seem bizarre? It did to me. I felt like something weird was going to happen. Goosebumps crept up my arms. Like, imagine that lady had gotten Bella kidnaped! That would be horrible. Or, what if she came and accused Bella of stealing her necklace so she could sue her and become a millionaire? I shuddered. I had heard too many such crazy stories, and they scared me. I never want to get sued, though I don't think I would mind suing someone. Ha-ha.

"Okay, okay. Go on!" I said, despite my doubts.

"So she took the necklace from my hand and opened up the clasp. But then, the weirdest thing happened. The second she touched it, a strange type of red fog formed in the crystal," Bella continued.

"What!?" I yelled.

"I know!" Bella exclaimed. "It came out of nowhere, and the longer she held it, the redder it got. It was so weird. I asked her what that was all about, and she smiled. She smiled. It was super creepy. I almost ran away from her, but I didn't want to hurt her feelings. Oh, and get this. She said that it was magic. Magic. Can you believe that? She said the longer I wear it, the more magical I will get and the more things I can achieve. But she said that, for it to work, I can never, ever take it off. It used to be hers but, apparently, it does not work on her anymore, and she does not need it. I mean, it's just so... so amazing! To think that magic truly exists!"

"Bella, I would not... I mean, it's beautiful and all, but I do not think you should keep it on forever. This does not feel right. You get me?" I smiled uneasily, then continued, "I mean, I'm super happy that you got such a beautiful necklace, but it sounds so eerie. First, an old woman shows up and tells you that this thing is your, and her, savior. Then this weird fog... I mean... it sounds so strange. As your best friend, I will do everything I am capable of doing to protect you like you have been doing all your life for me. Don't you think it's a bit strange that she said it was magic? Even if she isn't lying, there are different types of magic, you know. The good kind and the evil kind. My gut is telling me this is the evil kind."

"No. I do not think it is strange at all. I think this is amazing, and it's the most luck I've had since, like, forever, Amber. It's such a beautiful—no—enchanting necklace. I love it! And I want it to turn redder than when it was in the hands of the old lady. I already told Mom that I want this necklace forever and ever and that this is my most treasured gift. She promised never ever to let it get lost, Amber. Magic!" Bella repeated without taking a breath. It seemed that the word "magic" had gotten to her.

"I know, I know. But still..." I said, staring at her

crazed expression warily. I wasn't feeling right about this and, to be honest, I didn't mind arguing about it. It was distracting me from my troubles and, unlike some other people, I liked being distracted.

"Still, nothing. I am going to call this 'the Skull-full Skulled-filled Sword-filled Heart,'" she said, and we giggled at the title. "Try saying that twenty-five times really fast!" she exclaimed.

I shook my head. "What did the lady call it?" I inquired.

After a moment of thinking, Bella answered, "The Heart of Time."

I laughed. "Ooooh, fancy!" I said.

"I know right?!" she said, nodding vigorously.

I smiled, stretching out.

"Let's have some fun tonight. How about that? It's been so long since we have actually had fun," Bella suggested as she skipped over to her iPod, smiling with delight. Her parents had gone to the grocery store and would not be back for at least half an hour.

"We get to live this life once. Let's have some fun while we still can," she said excitedly.

"Alright," I said. I felt a twang as I remembered my mom.

No, you will not dwell on that right now. Right now, you will have fun, I ordered myself.

I wanted to forget all the things that were happening.

Bella pressed a few buttons and, soon, her crazy dancing playlist was booming throughout the house, the volume on high.

She screamed as she took my hands in hers and twirled me around to "Shake It Off."

With the loud music around us, we did not even hear what was going on until, out of the blue, a loud rumble went through the house, and then there was nothing but darkness. The last thing I saw was a small red fog forming around the gem of the necklace that Bella wore. I had started to get a curious and suspicious feeling about the necklace. And it was a bad feeling...

Amidst the confusion of the times, the conflicts of conscience, and the turmoil of daily living, an abiding faith becomes an anchor to our lives.

Thomas S. Monson

Chapter THREE

"I do not know what to say," someone said with a teary voice.

I was in a box. I looked up and saw the sky.

What even… I thought to myself.

"These two young girls were the heart of my class," the same voice blabbed, her tears making her words break apart. She sounded a lot like Ms. Dennis, mine, and Bella's home room teacher at Glory Home Middle School. "The brightest, most amazing students. Such beautiful young souls they were, and it's so sad that they have left us."

What on Earth is going on? I wondered once again.

"Uh, hello!" I said, stretching the o. "What am I, invisible?" I was interrupted by Ms. Dennis, her voice shaking even more. As she started to talk, I heard horrible sobs that made me think, Maybe I am invisible…

The voice said, "Although I had the privilege of teaching them only this year, I knew Bella and Amber from the first time they stepped into Glory Home Middle School. I knew of the caring hearts they had. They always took care of others and did their best to be shining stars. And it hurts, it hurts so much to see that we lost two beautiful lives in such a tragic accident." It was Ms. Dennis, our homeroom teacher this year.

I sat up and saw a crowd of people—family, friends, teachers. Everyone I knew was there. However, all of them wore tear-stricken faces, and no one seemed to realize that I had sat up. Even though they were all looking straight at me, no one appeared to realize that I was staring right back at them. I looked at my surroundings and gasped. It looked like I was in a coffin.

41

I kid you not. When I turned around, I saw my body. My head was right where it had been when I was laying down. My face looked peaceful, but the sad frown and lines remained from the week of depression I had gone through after Mom's death. It was a sight I would never forget.

But… how is it possible that I am seeing myself? I wondered.

Am I dreaming?

Suddenly, at that moment, a rustle of the wind caused the leaves from a tree to swoosh side by side on their way to the ground.

And then something happened.

It was the weirdest thing. I would never forget the shock I felt at that moment…

The leaves went right through me.

Through me.

As if I did not exist. Like I was not even there.

As if I wasn't human, and I didn't belong in this world.

I tried pinching myself, but my fingers went right through me, too.

I was ready to freak out.

This has to be a dream; I told myself over and over again. But it didn't work. So I did the next best thing: I willed myself to wake up. I wrapped my arms around myself and repeated to myself over and over again: Wake up. Wake up. Wake up.

It was weird, my hands went through me, but I felt my hands around me as well.

Regardless, I didn't give up on that for a good two

minutes.

I had to wake up because this dream was going to give me a heart attack.

I tried shaking myself awake.

Nothing happened.

And then, at that moment, people rushed to where my... body... was, and where I was sitting. But, again, it was like I did not exist. Their hands went through me as they moved the leaves off of my body. Their eyes were full of sadness as they looked at me. Many looked like they had been crying. Some were still crying, and others seemed about to cry.

I gulped.

After a while, I felt a bit more confident. Summoning all my willpower, I slowly and cautiously got up and jumped down.

Nothing happened.

The dream didn't end, and the sad environment stayed as it was.

It was like I was both something and nothing at once. It scared me because, the longer I stayed, the more realistic the thought became that this was not a dream.

I walked over to my dad, who was sitting on a chair. Tears were streaming down his face. He was crying as much—if not harder—as he had when he found out Mom had died.

His eyes were bloodshot, and they told me that his heart was shattered as I had never, ever seen it before. His eyes were normally as hard as the strongest glass in the world, but right now, that strongest of glasses wasn't just cracked, it was completely shattered. I walked closer to him, trying to help him see that I was right there and that I wouldn't let anything make him cry again. But when put my hand on his shoulder, I was treated with complete nothingness.

No reaction.

"Stop ignoring me! This isn't funny!" I yelled right into my dad's ear.

He just continued to cry.

My chest felt tight. I felt like I was going to die. I wanted to cry with him, but I had no idea why he was even crying.

Then it hit me. Like when summer suddenly collapses into fall, the realization collapsed into my mind.

They were all here—everyone I knew. Everyone I loved and cared for. And even some of those that I thought hated me. Clara sat the very corner of the audience, a sorrowful shadow across her face. Her parents were on either side of her, holding her hands in each of theirs as they tried to calm her down.

I walked over to the casket. There were two bodies. One was me. The other… Bella.

I gulped.

I was… dead.

I gulped once again as I let it sink in.

It then occurred to me that I had to find out where Bella was. If I was a ghost, she must be a ghost, too, right? I could not see her. Well, I saw her body, but not a version of her that was awake, like me.

I turned back to my wailing dad, and my heart broke. I could not contain myself as a sob escaped through my mouth.

"My poor baby," Dad whispered in agony as he buried his face in his hands, and his voice broke as he looked over at the coffin where I lay.

My heart broke when I saw the look in his eyes. I bit back a sob at the same time as I heard a soft, "Hey."

Slowly, I turned around, half-expecting to see Bella, half-expecting that I was hallucinating and that no one had actually spoken. Or, probably, someone was here to talk to Dad.

But when I turned around, I gasped. For the first time, at that moment, someone was looking at me and treating me like I was actually there and not invisible. A short girl around my age stared straight at me. For the first time since I had… woken up, someone looked at me rather than right through me.

The petite girl, who looked to be my age, had long, golden locks and hazel-colored eyes. She smiled at my stunned face. What got my bones all stiff and cold was the fact that she was not like the rest of the people there. She was not… solid. There was something about her that seemed off. It looked like things could go through her as they went through me.

"It's okay," she said. She was as see-through as glass. Just like a ghost. Just like me. I could see right through her but could see her just the same.

"You can call me Sara. I am just like you," my fellow dead person said.

We cannot solve our problems with the same thinking we used when we created them.

Albert Einstein

Chapter FOUR

"L-like me? W-w-what do you m-mean?" I stuttered.

"Oh! I am so sorry; I should have explained all of this to you before I started talking nonsense. You must be pretty lost and confused right now, right?" the girl said, shaking her head in embarrassment.

I nodded hopelessly.

"My fault," she said. "I didn't know the complete details either, but I can tell you what I have heard from the other ghosts."

"Please, enlighten me," I said carefully, following her lead by sitting down on a rock. Thankfully, we didn't fall into it.

"Well, you died around... hmm... about three days ago. When your friend's house collapsed five days ago, people could not find you or your friend for almost two days. When they did, they took you both straight to the hospital, but the second you arrived, you both were pronounced dead. Anyway, something else happened around six days ago—something huge. The dead are no longer able to go to the afterlife. For the past six days, every dead person has been turned into a ghost and, for now, you and Bella are stuck in the in-between world with us. Just in case you do not know the meaning of that, let me tell you—THAT MEANS CHAOS! That means utter doom for all of us who have died. If whatever happened isn't fixed, we will never, ever be able to go to the afterlife!" Sara gushed. "And that means we will never, ever find out if we will go to Heaven or not..." she said with grave eeriness.

I gulped. Although what this girl was saying

sounded like it came out of a novel, she seemed trust-worthy. "What do we do? What happened? Where are all the ghosts?" I had a bad feeling about the six days part. Six days ago was when Mom had died. I felt my stomach turn inside out.

"I do not know, but I do know someone who might know what is going on. I heard she does not answer everyone's questions, but we can always try," Sara said. "Apparently, she has been in the Ghost World for years. No one knows how or why, but she has stayed here of her own will. She has the power to turn into human form whenever she likes, or to remain a ghost. But something has changed, and now she cannot do it anymore. Six days ago, she lost her power, and no one knows why. The second she lost her power, all of the dead stopped going to the afterlife. For now, all the ghosts are staying in Shadowfleet Graveyard," she said in a very creepy voice.

I always knew that Shadowfleet Graveyard was weird. "So when did you die?" I asked, unable to control my curiosity. I mean, if someone knows every single detail about you and what happened to you, you can't help but wonder everything about them.

She replied without missing a beat or shooting me a weird look for being nosy.

"It has been five days now. I have been trying to count, but it's kind of hard in the Ghost World."

"If you do not mind sharing, how exactly did you die?" I pestered.

"Oh! I should have said that. Sorry! I actually had cancer. I am not surprised that I ended up here, though. I was expecting it for a while. It hurts to know that my death has caused so many people pain, but it's made me feel so carefree and happy, you know? No pain from the cancer and stuff. Still, this new problem is such a pain in the neck. I want to get to Heaven and rest in peace with my Grandma and Grandpa. I am looking forward to it. The Mother of it All says she is only waiting for someone to save all the ghosts so that they can all go to Heaven," she said pretty excitedly. I had noticed that she was a generally excited person.

Excited, and ready to save the world. I could not even begin to think of how many people she must have affected when she was alive. I smiled for the first time since waking up as a ghost.

"Anyway, let's go kick some butts and solve this problem," she said excitedly.

I nodded. "Let's go," I said with a little less enthusiasm than her.

Then I said, staring at my hands, "Wait. I want to see our bodies one last time, to make sure this isn't a dream."

Sara nodded sympathetically. "I understand. It was hard for me to believe that I had woken up in a coffin."

Sara and I walked over to mine and Bella's coffins. How was one to feel when one found out one had died?

I looked over at Bella and her innocent face but gasped when I realized that the necklace I had seen around her neck was nowhere in sight. I scanned the crowd of people and could not see it anywhere. I remembered hearing her mother say something a few minutes ago about how they had wanted to bury her with the necklace because she loved it so much.

I looked at Bella once again, and that is when I started shaking in fear. Her face looked worse than before. Its innocence was lost. There was not even a speck of Bella left in the face I was looking at.

I knew she was truly dead. I looked away. It was too painful to see Bella, my best friend, like that. I went to my coffin and looked in. My face was also pale, scary and, well—dead. I gulped back the sob that was stuck in my throat.

"I'm sorry," Sara said, her face ashen. "Let's go." I was glad to leave the scary scene.

A hero is an ordinary individual who finds the strength to persevere and endure in spite of overwhelming obstacles.

Christopher Reeve

Chapter FIVE

"Where are we going?" I asked Sara.

"Underground, to Ghost Alley," Sara replied.

"There is a place called Ghost Alley?" I asked, astonished that the Ghost World had developed so quickly.

"Six days ago, no. But now, the Ghost Alley is the only place that us ghosts have. So many people die every day that it didn't take too long for Ghost Alley to come about."

I might have looked scared. Maybe that was why Sara offered a soft smile and kind words.

"Don't worry, girl, we got this! We are going to go and, eventually, get to the afterlife. No matter what it takes, I will do my best to help you whenever I can. A ghost's vow." She gently smiled, raising her right hand formally.

"No matter what it takes," I repeated. "So, how many ghosts are there?"

"To be honest, I do not know myself," Sara said. "But I did overhear someone say that about two people on Earth die every second of every minute of every hour of every day of every week of every month! So, I did the math and all those ugly calculations. I figured that around 120 people die per minute. 7,200 people per hour. 172,800 people per day and, because today is like the sixth day of this horrible thing, there should be around 1,036,800 ghosts in Ghost Alley so far," explained Sara matter-of-factly, counting off on her fingers. It was like she had been memorizing these details for years.

"Wow... That is a lot!" I exclaimed.

"And it's only increasing! Now, let's go!" she said

worriedly.

Sara led me through different roads and paths until we finally reached Shadowfleet Graveyard. "Please, not in there," I gulped.

"I am afraid so. It's right there. Now let's go! We do not have time!" Sara said.

I hesitantly followed her into the graveyard. The second we stepped in, it was like I was in an arcade of ghosts. Thousands of ghosts swooshed back and forth in haste. Sara weaved through the crowd until we were right in front of a big hole by a big, creepy tree with branches that looked like claws and features that only a monster could muster.

"Now, we jump!" she said enthusiastically. Her face showed different shades of excitement.

"Are you crazy?!" I cried. "I am NOT jumping in there!"

"Oh, come on! It's so much fun, trust me. We need to get to Ghost Alley and ask the Mother of It All what we can do to help! In you, I've finally found someone who I feel like I can trust. You seem like you can change everything for the better. Please, Amber, we all need you," Sara said.

Oh God! I thought. How do I get out of this?!

"No! No way! I will not... Ewww! Look at all of that muck and mud and dust and dirt! It looks disgusting! No way am I going down there," I said disgustedly. I crossed my arms in defiance. Sara groaned in protest. There was no way something like this Ghost Alley could be in there. Ghosts should have some sort of class, no?

"Oh come on! Stop acting like a scared baby princess

cat! Just try it at least once. If you do not like it, I will take you back up or down the other way! It will be fun this way! You will even get to experience how a feather feels when it is falling! It's sensational," Sara giggled.

I always got stuck in the most dangerous, detrimental situations. "Okay," I said nonetheless.

On the count of three, we both jumped into the hole and went down, down, down.

It was such a deep hole, but it was so much fun. Already I felt lightweight—I had ever since I became a ghost—and sliding down the hole made me feel like I was literally nothing.

"Woohoo!!!" We both screamed until we got to the very bottom.

We giggled once we got to our feet. The thought hit me, just like a rocket ship at full speed, that sometimes the smallest things can mean the most.

We high-fived each other, and I realized that I had made an actual, real, true friend who was a ghost. In less than, what, ten minutes? Sara was right, it was hard to keep track of time as a ghost. For the first time, I had gotten out of the Bella-Amber bond that I had taken with me everywhere and become friends with someone new. To tell you the truth, although I loved Bella just as much as I always had, I was loving making new friends. I was not very good at making friends at the time.

A little while ago, I had felt so alone. But now, I felt like the weight and confusion on my shoulders was shared with someone else, and I felt safe.

"Ready?" Sara asked.

"Ready," I replied.

"Alright! So, I suggest you do not try to talk to any of the ghosts. Most of them are pretty grumpy and upset because their numbers keep increasing, and there does not seem to be any solution. They are in trouble, especially because none of them wants to do anything. They're just sitting and lounging around Shadowfleet Graveyard's Alley like the solution is going to walk right up to them. Stupid ghosts," Sara said, shaking her head. She glared at a ghost beside them, who was slouching and calling out, "Who is working on the answer to this problem?"

"Well, whoever wants to," Sara muttered. "which is pretty much just a handful of people."

"That is awful!" I said.

Well, now I am one of them, I thought to myself.

"I know! That is why you and I are here! We are going to get us out of this mess and figure this out together." Sara said.

"So where does the Mother of it All stay?" I asked.

"Well, The Mother of it All, that is what most people call her, actually has her own room smack in the center of Ghost Alley, and all the ghosts go to her for help of all kinds. She can give us a solution to our problem as quickly as the speed of time!" she said.

People change and forget to tell each other.

Lillian Hellman

Chapter SIX

On our way to The Mother of it All's "headquarters," Sara's words were shown to be true. Most of the ghosts were just lounging around. There were so many that I could not help but worry about how I would find Bella or my mom.

The thought had just crossed my mind when I suddenly shouldered another ghost that was the same height as me. She looked very familiar. It was Bella, and she had a small group of ghosts trailing behind her. They immediately stopped and whipped their heads around.

"Bella?!" I squealed happily. Sara stopped walking and quietly stood behind me.

Bella turned her head and looked at me. However, she did not seem as happy to see me as I was to see her.

"How dare you bump into me?!" she asked in a rage.

I took a step back. My heart sped rapidly in my chest, and the desire to cry climbed up into my throat and my eyes.

"I—I did not see you. Sorry!" I said in embarrassment and confusion.

"Well, are you that blind, that you could not see? You totally need some glasses, young lady—to make you look like a dork!" she seethed.

I almost giggled at what her group did next. When she said 'glasses,' 'blind,' and 'dork,' they said it with her, and as they said it, they twirled around—a 360-degree turn—then rolled their eyes at me. If I wasn't so hurt, I would've laughed.

"Bella, what is wrong with you?" I asked in a pained voice.

"Nothing is wrong with me," she said curtly.

"Bella, we are best friends. It's me, Amber Williams. Did you forget that? And where did you go? I could not find you at our funeral. And that neckl—" I cut my sentence short when I saw the rage growing and growing on her face.

Bella was not happy to see me, and it hurt like a great pang in my chest. There I was, worrying my neck off about where she could be, and now that I had found her, she just seemed to be angry at me.

Was it something I said? I wondered.

Bella usually forgave me in a second when I bumped into her. Maybe she was just grumpy. I mean, most of the ghosts were. No one wanted to be here. I couldn't blame her for being angry. But what really got to me was when I saw her necklace. It was around her neck, and the gem was starting to get redder and redder.

I gulped.

Did the necklace have something to do with her behavior?

I brushed the thought aside.

She is just upset. She is just grumpy; I chided myself.

I guessed that she also must be confused. Finding out that you had died, become a ghost, and that none of your family members were with you was pretty scary stuff. Believe me, I would know. Hey, I went through all that stuff too.

"I need to go," Bella said as she eyed me. I nodded and looked down at her necklace once more. It had turned a still darker shade of red. I shuddered and felt a suspicion. I was scared at what was happening to my dear friend Bella.

"Okay, but I am here for you, Bella, if you need me. We are best friends, remember?" I asked. It felt weird to remind her of our relationship with each other, but I felt like it was necessary. The way she was behaving made it seem like we weren't friends, or even strangers, but enemies. And I did not like that idea at all.

But, God, nothing could've prepared me for what Bella said next. My suspicions were correct.

"Nooo! No, no, no, no, no, no! We are not best friends, Amber. We were best friends. We are not anymore. You are not like me anymore. You are different, and you will always stay that way!" With that and a flip of her hair, she walked away haughtily. Her group of ghosts followed right behind her, laughing and whispering. I had a sneaking suspicion about what—or rather who—they were talking about.

"I am not the one who is different now, Bella, you are," I whispered as a tear went down my cheek. I jumped when Sara appeared in front of me. She had been so quiet that I had almost forgotten she was there.

"Hey, do not worry about her. Do not take what she said to heart, Amber. She's just… sad, like all the other ghosts," Sara said. She mirrored a sad face, and I could see pity in her eyes. "Let's go."

I wiped away a tear and nodded as I followed her.

"People just seem to get really upset when they enter the Ghost World. As you can see, this isn't exactly the place one would want to be after they die," Sara said.

"I can tell," I replied with a nod.

"Almost there," she said cheerfully.

A few minutes later, we stood in front of a creepy black castle-ish place. It had sharp edges and what looked like claws on top. "Why is everything around here creepy?" I whispered to Sara.

"Probably because we are all ghosts," Sara replied with a little smile as we strolled into the castle. Sara seemed to have been here before as she skillfully guided the two of us to The Mother of it All's room. "Call her The Mother of it All. Nothing else." Sara sounded as if she felt sorry for me because of what had just happened.

I nodded and loudly swallowed as Sara knocked on the door.

A blood-churning waiver of a voice called out to us. It was soft and high pitched, profound and dark, but also smooth in a creepy way, as well as calculated and raspy.

"Come in Amber, Sara." The Mother of it All said.

*The good and bad things are what form us as people...
Change makes us grow.*

Kate Winslet

Chapter SEVEN

"Hello, dear. I was expecting you," The Mother of it All said the second we entered. She was a timeworn lady, transparent like the rest of the ghosts. She had gray hair and steel-gray eyes that looked right at me. But she was different. There was a glint in her look that did something to my heart. A shiver ran down my spine when I saw her.

I gulped. I was feeling oddly shy all of a sudden. "I am A—" I started hesitantly.

"Amber. Yes, I know. And I have been waiting for you," The Mother of it All said with a smile. She had parched, thin lips like thin strips of paper. She wore ragged clothes covered with ashes—it looked like she had died from a fire. Gray strands of thread—which she would probably have called hair—dangled from her scalp. I stared at her humongous eyes, which gave her a kind look. Her smile lit up her fair skin tone. She had long, sharp, and pointy teeth. They seemed yellow and plaque-y.

Ewww.

Well, in the Ghost World, I bet you have more important things to think about than brushing your teeth.

Nonetheless, I nodded my head once, rather stiffly, to acknowledge her. I gulped so loudly that I was sure the whole world could hear me. And my booming heart did not help the situation.

"I am sure Sara has informed you of the circumstances that have been occurring here," The Mother of it All started.

I nodded my head again. I felt so stiff that it barely moved. Again, I was unable to speak.

"Dear, you can talk to me. I do not bark at those who talk," she said, with another little smile that made her eyes sparkle.

I stared at her, then blushed, embarrassed.

"S-sorry," I stuttered. I slightly shook my head, afraid she would chop it off, even though I was already dead.

"It's okay," The Mother of it All said. She looked at me, judging me carefully. I could see it in her eyes and in the slight tilt of her head.

"Amber, I have chosen you to fix this problem. I see purity in you. You have the power to change people and the world. I am trusting you with this mission. Do you think you can do it?" The Mother of it All asked. Her confidence in me sparked confidence within myself.

For the first time in my life—no, existence—I felt special and unique. I felt like a hero without whom the world would break. And the reality was, I really was a hero—well, not yet, but I was soon to be a hero. The reality of it sunk in when I realized that it wasn't just the dead who needed my help to get to the afterlife. Even I needed my help.

"Yes, I can," I said with newfound confidence. My voice was louder than I meant it to be, and my eyes widened as The Mother of it All gave me a startled look.

"Perfect!" she replied nonetheless, with equal enthusiasm.

"But I have a few questions. Do you know exactly what triggered the passage to the afterlife to close?" I asked.

"Actually, yes I do," The Mother of it All said. "You

see, there is a powerful object by the name of the Heart of Time. It's a magical necklace with a crystal-clear circular gem. The gem has intricate designs on the glass that look like the little gears you would typically find in a watch. The edges of the gem have a beautiful design of skulls and swords. And…"

"And?" I gulped, interrupting her speech. I knew exactly what she was talking about, and it was killing me. My face reddened in fear.

"And it turns red upon…" The Mother of it All paused, eyeing me carefully. Her eyes started to pop out, abruptly and in a frightened way. They turned red.

"Upon?" Sara and I asked simultaneously.

"Upon evil," The Mother of it All finished. I had to struggle to keep myself from gasping and freaking out over the news. "The slightest element of evil—hatred, jealousy, pain, pride, gluttony, anger, greed, selfishness, rudeness, lying—any act or feeling with a bad and negative meaning leads the gem to become redder and redder. And the redder the Heart of Time becomes, the more lives are at stake in this world, in the afterlife, and in death. Also, remember this: if it gains a speck of red for even a millisecond, the red spot will only grow bigger afterward. It will turn a much bolder, richer, and bloodier color of red. It forces the person wearing it do evil, whether or not that person wants to. You cannot ever take the necklace off. Only if the wearer faces something or someone that they love, or some other form of positive feeling—which will differ depending on the person—and battles the evil within himself or herself, will the darkness leave. Only then will the red fog in the gem subside, and the gem will become entirely clear. Then, and only then, is the person able to take off the necklace," she said.

I gulped.

This explained everything!

Everything Bella had done, and the things she had said, made sense. The small things she had gotten upset at. Her lie to her mom. Suddenly, it all clicked. It was the Heart of Time the whole time!

"But... How do you know all this?" I asked. "I mean, with all due respect, no one else—the ghosts, the humans, anyone in Heaven—no one else seems to have knowledge of all this, except you. Why?"

The Mother of it All laughed a very high-pitched laugh. "Clever girl, you are," she said. Then she immediately sobered up as she told me one of the weirdest stories I had ever heard in my life—I mean, death. "Amber, this 'in-between' life isn't easy to understand. You see, the Heart of Time isn't just a very powerful gem. It's a chain that connects life—the living world—with the afterlife. It's also a chain that ties a pure heart to the in-between life. Without a pure heart holding the string, everything goes haywire—the afterlife is blocked. I would know because... because I was the Keeper for the past several centuries. I had the necklace bound to my neck, and I had to sit here for years and years to allow others to pass by. I had to sacrifice myself. I could not see Heaven." She paused and sighed thoughtfully. I could almost see her imagining paradise.

"I did not get to relax. Instead, I spent years by myself, without a single being in my presence. And it felt so horrible and lonely. I could not take it anymore. So, for the first time in ten centuries, I changed form and became human. I gave the necklace to someone who I believed had a pure heart. We have the power to do that, but once we do it, we risk the safety of the whole afterlife system. Anyway, I thought this girl was pure, someone who would be able to handle what I had gone through for so long, so… I gave her the necklace. And I lied to her. It was not right, I know it was not! I did not mean to, but it just happened. And I did not realize that something that started with a lie was evil in itself. That girl is no longer pure, and I got her killed. The Heart of Time is so powerful that it can take away life from someone who has not died, and it has weird ways of doing it. I do not even have the ability to see her because I gave up all my powers. And the girl, she now has the authority to hide immediately from whoever she wants. The necklace automatically protects its bearer from the previous owner—which is me," The Mother of it All heaved an exasperated breath. The poor old lady.

"I have been waiting for a pure heart, and I see it in you. I need you to find that girl. I wish I could give you a picture of the Heart of Time, but nothing like that exists. I just hope my description was good enough. I need you to find the girl, and then I will give you information on what you have to do next. Amber, do you think you can do it? Do you think you can save us all and help us get through to the afterlife?" The Mother of it All asked me.

Could I fight with my best friend and change everything once and for all?

I nodded. "I will die trying," I said with unbreakable determination.

"No offense, but you're already dead, Amber," Sara said, raising an eyebrow.

"Oh… right. But you get what I am saying. I will do everything in my power to fix everything," I said, scratching my head, embarrassed.

"I do not expect any less from you, Amber, dear. We need you to finish this!" The Mother of it All said with a big smile that made her eyes crinkle with delight.

After wishing The Mother of it All well, Sara and I left the castle and walked amongst the many other ghosts. We both walked quietly, not talking to each other or anyone else. We just watched and looked frantically for Bella. I did not need to explain anything to Sara because she knew of the secret that I had not told The Mother of it All.

When we were finally exhausted from searching, we sat on one of the ghost benches. Sara broke the silence.

"It's her, isn't it?" she asked.

I nodded quietly.

"So what are you going to do?" Sara asked.

"I am going to try to find her, first, and then talk to her. I want to help her out of this mess," I said with determination.

"Is she a friend?" Sara asked, holding my hand.

"Best friend," I answered quietly. Sara hugged me sympathetically.

"Oh," was all she could muster at the news.

You collect people to take with you. Some people change, other people don't... It's wonderful because I've met some incredible friends.

Imogen Poots

Chapter EIGHT

"Well, from the looks of what Bella has done now, I do not think this is going to end well, Sara," I said, shaking my head at the misfortunate events unfolding.

I watched Bella in the distance. She was punching and kicking ghosts, stepping on their feet, and insulting children—this was not like Bella.

I watched as the children, along with their parents, moved away from Bella and into the surrounding area. Others shuffled as Bella hurt or insulted them. A few broke down in tears and hugged their elders. Some of larger ghosts could've been parents to the little ones.

I felt a sudden ache in my heart and wanted to cry. I had yet to find my mom.

My best friend, the girl who I knew would never, ever do wrong, was standing in front of me and harming dead people she did not know—I mean, does that even make sense? Little did she know that she was only doing harm to herself.

Bella's innocent-looking face, which I had grown so fond of over the years, had disappeared. In its place, she had an expression of anger, depression, sadness, and torment. But there was also a glint in her eye that showed she was actually enjoyed this. Sara, seeing this, assured me that it was just the Heart of Time at work. But, Heart of Time or no Heart of Time, I could not stand the sadness in Bella's eyes.

Bella stomped away from the kids, grunting something. "Stupid people," she said as she pushed me with her shoulder for no reason, walking right by like I was a stranger. I noticed how her necklace glowed bright red. Redder than before. Blood-red.

This is not good, I thought, raking a hand through my hair.

But how was I supposed to get her to listen to me?

Bella was now ignoring me even more—if possible—than she had been before. She was actually losing her mind from all the negativity in this horrid Ghost World.

I stared at the ground thoughtfully, hand on chin. I had to figure out a way to turn this Bella back into my Bella. The girl who would stop everything she was doing to greet me. The girl who would help anyone, even if they didn't want or need it. The girl who used to stand up to bullies. Now—in this wretched Ghost World—Bella was the bully.

Sara tugged me to her, and throughout that whole day, I sadly watched as Bella's behavior worsened. She became meaner and meaner and harsher and harsher and so, so rude. Many times, I wanted to walk over to her and angrily lecture her about how wrong and evil this was, but it was too hard. It was so hard to look into the cold, sad eyes that I used to look into with happiness.

At one point, Bella pushed a baby ghost to the ground. At first, my mouth was agape. Despite all of this stupid Heart of Time stuff, I would never have expected her to push a baby—that couldn't walk, mind you—to the ground. Then my face turned red in anger. Why on Earth would anyone push a poor baby on the ground when it is literally already crawling on the ground? And without a second thought, fuming, I walked over to Bella and clenched her arm in my hands. Hard. I could feel my nails dig into her arm, and I finally spoke, throwing all my anger at her.

"What is wrong with you, Bella?!" I yelled.

Sara screamed, "Amber, get back here!"

I could've punched Bella right there, but I knew that even if I raised my fist to do that, I would immediately put it down. I couldn't look into those blue eyes I had known so well and punch her. It would be close to impossible. But I was still angry, and if I couldn't attack her physically, I would do it with my words.

"What has gotten into you?" I continued, shaking her, a wild look in my eyes. I saw Bella's mean smile flicker and her eyes show a little fear. "You were never like this before! Why are you doing this? What have you done to the Bella I know? Bella! The real one! You had better wake up! Stop letting yourself be ruled by the evil. You are a good person. You are the kindest person I know. You have always been one of the good guys. Don't let evil take you away. Bella, I am begging you to stop changing," I continued, pleading. I felt my eyes burn as I pulled my hands away from her arms.

Bella glared at me in disgust and rubbed her arms—which my nails had accidentally dug into. She looked at me like I was a stranger. Like she had no idea who I was. The look in her eyes no longer held fear, but only more anger than before.

"Who are you?" she asked. The way she said it, you'd have thought she was throwing every ounce of anger at me that she had ever had for anyone in her life. Like I was the bad guy or something!

I gulped and held back my tears. My best friend didn't know me.

"I—I'm Amber. We are best friends. At least, I think

we are," I said, close to tears. I was a bit taken back by the shock.

Bella looked me over and, by the looks of it, she didn't like what she saw. She glared haughtily at me. "No, we are not. We might've been best friends before, but now, you are not worthy," she said coolly.

"Bella, please stop. You don't know what you're saying," I cried, desperately trying to reason with her.

"I know what I'm saying. I always know what I'm saying," she said, haughtily, hands on hips. "Now, get out of my face before I ruin you forever. I'm not in the mood to deal with stupid brats like you. I'm already feeling so restless because we can't rest in peace."

With that, Bella stuck her tongue out at me and pushed me so roughly that I fell to the floor. It hurt—not physically, but emotionally. My best friend had pushed me, and she didn't even turn back to look at me. With determination coursing through my blood, I jumped up and started to run after Bella, but Sara held me back.

"Stop! Amber, stop right now!" I felt Sara's scream vibrate and echo in my stomach.

I looked at her painfully. I shook my head. Tears began to drop, one by one.

"Look at what she has become," I wailed. "She has become such a monster that—" I started to tremble. "—that even I cannot control her anymore," I cried.

"It isn't you, Amber. It's the Heart of Time. And besides, you have done all you could to help her," Sara said, pulling me into an embrace. But that just made me cry more because it reminded me of Bella's motherly hugs. Sara's eyes held sympathy as she gazed into mine.

"Did you look at her, though?" I asked. "People are scared of her. She does the opposite of what she used to do," I said, trembling. I pulled out of Sara's embrace and buried my face in my hands.

"Listen. Never, ever give up." Sara sighed. "Please don't give up. There is a solution to everything. We will save Bella. We will help Bella become good again, no matter what it takes. For the time being, all we can do is not give up." Sara held my gaze for a moment, then smiled determinedly. "I know you can do it. You have been proving to me how strong you are ever since we met. I know you will remain strong."

And for the first time in a while, I remembered my mother's words: "You will always find people who give you trouble in life, but never, ever give up. You are a ray of sunshine, my dear. Shine on whatever you can, and shine as long as the sun is up."

As we stood in the middle of the crowd, discussing this before everyone, I saw some ghosts looking at me like they felt sorry for me. I didn't like that. I liked to think of myself as a hero that helped others and who people looked at with happiness. I didn't want to be a weak girl that needed to be saved.

"Thanks, Sara," I said, brushing away tears. My voice came out a little scratchy. I cleared my throat and said, "I'm positive we will save her."

Sara hugged me again, the two of us still on the ground, then helped me up, mumbling incoherent words of comfort.

"Let's go, Amber. Let's figure out what we will do to help Bella together," Sara said, fist-bumping me.

Music connects us. Something wonderful happens.

Armin Van Buuren

Chapter NINE

Sara and I went on a break after my little outburst and stopped following Bella around—only for a while of course. Instead, we walked over to the ghost beach to sit down on the cool sand and plan what we would do and how we could help get Bella to see the positive candle of light in the dark room of evil she had accidentally entered.

"Again, Amber, I'm sorry about what Bella said. She didn't mean it. It wasn't her. It was the necklace. You understand, right?" Sara said.

I nodded without a word.

"Don't give up on her, okay?"

"Oh, I'm not going to give up. I will never give up. We are going to solve this and help all the ghosts get where they belong," I said, defiantly crossing my arms. Sara's smile stretched a mile.

"Yes, that's the spirit, girl! That's exactly what I wanted to hear," Sara said with a hearty laugh. "I'm so happy you weren't discouraged. For a second there, I thought you would give up. What Bella said wasn't very nice, but she was not herself, so you really can't blame her."

I nodded slowly. "You know why Bella got attacked by the necklace? She had a pure heart. She was a completely good girl, but she lied. And she was hiding secrets. That was the first time she did that, and that small evil… it ruined her."

"Wow. That sucks. I guess people are right when they say that one act of evil leads to another. Her small act of evil resulted in the activation of the evil in the Heart of Time, and it made her continue doing bad things. Just pull the string a little bit, and everything unravels," Sara noted.

"Sadly, that is correct," I said with a sigh.

We stayed quiet for a while, each of us deep in our own thoughts.

"So what's the plan?" Sara asked, breaking the silence.

"I don't know…" I said, staring off at the sea. I looked up to her slowly. "Do you have any ideas?"

"Not really," she said, her eyebrows furrowing in thought. After a while, she sat up straight quickly and looked at me, her eyes flickering with excitement as she cried out, "Maybe if you try to get her to remember her good days, if you try to get her to understand that she was a good person, always has been, and always shall be, maybe she can break the spell and escape the evil of the Heart of Time."

"That's not a bad idea—" I said, but then I remembered that day's—um—incident and said, "Don't you think that's the same thing I tried today?"

"No. Well, sort of, but not exactly. You told her that she wasn't like that, but you didn't show her. Maybe you should give some specific examples of what she done, and see if that does any good."

"Good idea. Maybe it'll open up her heart," I said. Sara beamed with delight.

"Maybe. So that's our plan for tomorrow, okay?" Sara confirmed.

"Yes!" I nodded in agreement.

We looked at each other with joy. Maybe we could really do this. Maybe we could actually save the ghosts and rest in peace.

"Thank you, Sara," I said. "I don't think I would've been able to keep moving or remain sane without your help."

"Hey! No need to get all emotional. We are friends, and that's what friends are for. Let's get this thing going and save the world!" Sara said, patting my back good-naturedly.

After a while, I asked Sara if it would be okay for me to walk alone and think. As expected, she cheerfully encouraged it. She was like a psychologist in a little girl's body—her parents must've raised her in a very empathetic way.

Anyway, as I walked, I went as far away from the crowd as possible. I wanted to be able to breathe and think and collect myself.

Thankfully, I found a small forest. No one was there except for a small group of ghosts hanging around at the entrance.

I made my way through the trees and bushes and then sat down on a big rock next to a little pond.

For some reason, I started humming a tune. It was a song that Bella and I had written and sung for a girl who got bullied by Henry, a mean kid at our school. She was very insecure and didn't think she could stand up to him. Bella and I felt awful for her situation and wanted to help her. So we decided to put our support in the form of a song.

I felt like I was back in kindergarten, on the stage at the talent show. Bella and I had attended Welsby Preschool, which was a kindergarten, pre-kindergarten, and elementary school. We were holding hands and flashing our smile full of gaps at everyone.

The images flashed in my brain. Hundreds and hundreds of people were whispering and talking and staring at us in amused excitement. Bella and I were backstage watching the people through the curtains.

Our principal, Mrs. Margaret, took the stage and said, "The next group we have is a duet. They have done an excellent job practicing. They have made up a very special song, all by themselves, called 'Warrior.' And once again, they have practiced with all their hearts and put a lot of effort to the song. I have witnessed their hard work and sat through several meetings' to help make it perfect! So please give them all of your attention! Please welcome with lots of applause, Amber, and Bella, with 'Warrior!'" Mrs. Margaret left the stage and gave us the signal to let the curtains rise.

I still remember how I spoke into the microphone and said, "Ehm! Can I please get your attention? This song is dedicated to Debbie for her fight. Be strong, girl! You got this!" Lots of people clapped, and there were hundreds of flashes, which went on and on until we finished.

With a nod to each other, we began singing. And, with that memory, I couldn't control myself. I started singing to myself as I sat on the rock.

"There's only one person, you can trust.
She is the one inside you that you must, figure out.
It's hard to find her.
But she is inside.

She'll come when she is most,
Needed, needed
And she is going to rise from the Earth
And she is going to rise to the sky,
And she is going to teach you how to fly.
How to fly."

"Wh—who is there?!" someone cried. Someone familiar.

Immediately, I stopped singing and turned to the source of the voice. Bella was standing in front of me. Her necklace seemed to be a lighter shade of red than it was before. I almost gasped in surprise. After a long time, I saw a hint of kindness in her eyes and, for a second, I almost believed that the girl who was standing before me was the ever-harmless Bella.

"Hey…" I said awkwardly. I didn't know what else to say until I remembered her question. "It's me, Amber. Your best friend."

"Best friend? Ha! I don't have a best friend. Especially not someone like you," she said. I was so confused. Her eyes and her voice betrayed her words. I later found out that the necklace forced her to do everything. She was helpless before the Heart of Time. She could only watch as it did what it wanted.

"I know that song," Bella said quietly. I'm sure that, the second she said those words, my eyes lit up. She remembered! She remembered!

"We made that song up together, remember?"

"Yes… you didn't do anything," she said and, after a while, continued, "Oh my God! I can't control this, I swear... I'm the most powerful person ever."

She was fighting it!

"Bella, you can do it. Keep fighting it. You're not bad; you're good. You can do it!" I said eagerly, and I thought I had done it.

Then, suddenly, she looked at me with pure disgust. Her necklace grew a darker shade of red. "You stay away from me!" she shouted and, with that, she stomped away.

But two thoughts remained: one, she remembered! And two, she was fighting back. She was fighting her own battle.

But it didn't seem like it was enough.

For some reason, as I went back to find Sara, I decided not to tell her about the incident. Maybe it was a gut feeling. Maybe I was just being selfish. But for some reason, I wanted to keep the information to myself.

And I did.

If you don't sacrifice for what you want, what you want will be the sacrifice.

Sukh Sandhu

Chapter TEN

For a while, we walked around and relaxed. Sara was already exhausted from running after Bella for the whole day and, because ghosts don't sleep, we had no choice but to lounge around until we felt better.

But when we were sitting down, I noticed one thing that worried me—the ghosts were multiplying like crazy. There were so many ghosts that it was getting really crowded. They seemed to be walking right through each other, which did a weird thing to them—they shuddered and moved away. It was kind of silly because it reminded me of what happened when I tried to calm myself down by hugging myself. I felt the hug, but my hands went through. It looked painful, so I didn't even want to try. I guess, it was just like that, their bodies went through and they felt it go through as well.

Anyway, after a bit of relaxing, we decided that if we didn't start hunting Bella down and helping her to escape the evil, it might be too late. It would also become harder to find her.

And right we were. It took us hours of searching before we saw another large crowd of ghosts crying and screaming. Bella was up to no good. Sara and I ran over to talk to her. What we saw sent an ache through my heart. I had honestly thought that maybe, because of the song and because of her memories, she would stop. But I guess she was losing the battle inside herself.

Bella was screaming and hurting people, and she even purposely walked through the younger ghosts. And that's what surprised me—as she walked through the ghosts, she was unaffected. Nothing happened to her. But the other people, they flinched, and some even cried out in pain. I also noticed that though everyone fought back, whether by screaming or pushing back or just cursing her, she was unaffected by their blows. She didn't care. If anything, she was meaner to them because of their resistance.

As Bella was leaving this crowd to move on to another, I ran up to her and put a hand on her elbow. "Bella, can we please ta—" I was cut short and flinched upon touching her. Her body was full of evil. She had so much power. She looked at me and laughed mercilessly at my condition.

I was so close to crying—this was not Bella. This is not her. Then, a flood of memories flowed through me. I remembered what my mom said before the car crash; I remembered what Sara said about never giving up. I stood up straighter.

I cleared my throat and started again, "Bella, can we please talk?"

"Nope, I've got no time for you."

"Bella, listen, we ne—" And then I got cut off again.

"You!" someone yelled. It was a young girl who didn't look too happy. "You, I'm going to hurt you... you monster!" she screamed as she came up to Bella and pushed her down.

I stepped aside, afraid that I might get hurt.

"What in the world..." was all Bella got out. There was fury in her eyes as she tumbled to the floor.

"How dare you, how dare you hurt my sister?" the girl. She had blonde hair, green eyes, and a pretty sturdy body. She looked like one of those girls who went to the gym, could box, had a black belt in karate, and all those tom-boy things. But most of all... She. Looked. Angry.

"I dare everything," Bella said angrily, "but how dare you touch me like that?!"

The Heart of Time was throbbing red! And Bella no longer looked like Bella. "You dare to challenge me?!" she said, and with that, her hands spread out and fire burst out of them. At that moment, I couldn't help but feel hopeless. There was no way I could defeat her. I was as confused as ever at witnessing such supernatural things. The goal of saving all these ghosts and helping them rest in peace remained in my mind. Unfortunately, I lost hope in myself and of ever helping us.

Faster than anyone could react, Bells threw a fireball at the girl. Though it went right through her, it left a hole in her body, and she looked like she was in a lot of pain. What surprised me was that nothing seemed to kill the ghosts. They were ghosts, and I guess because they, I mean we, are already dead, everything and anything can happen, we can feel it, but there is no limit. You would feel pain forever and extreme amounts of it, but never be granted death.

Bella was about to throw another fireball. I don't know what came over me, but I heard my mother's words: "You will always find people who give you trouble in life, but never, ever give up. You are a ray of sunshine, my dear. Shine on whatever you can, and shine as long as the sun is up." And the sun was still up. The thought spread like a wildfire in my veins. I ran, stood right in front of the blonde, and stared straight into Bella's furious eyes.

When her eyes connected with mine, and she stared

at me, something changed. Her hands were still in attack mode, and one of them was ready to jab a fireball, but she looked guilty as soon as she let it go. It zoomed past me and almost hit my shoulder. Her hand wouldn't stop, I thought, until she threw a fireball right through me. But when her hand rose again to throw the ball, something clicked in her mind, and everything shut down. Her whole body collapsed, and the red in the Heart of Time decreased so much that I could only see a little pinkish fog remaining.

I gasped in surprise and ran, ran, ran to my best friend.

"Bella!" I cried as I dropped down next to her. "What happened to her??!" I asked. No one knew. Rather, no one could even breathe. Everyone was confused and scared. Thankfully, Sara was there to bring everyone back to life.

She got everyone's attention and helped the crowd move along as I tried getting Bella to wake up.

"Help me," Bella said weakly. She sounded like her old self. Her kind, non-furious self. I grabbed her hand and helped her sit up.

"Bella? How are you feeling?" I asked her.

"Amber, help me take it off!" she cried. But as I went to pull the necklace off, she yelled, "Don't touch me, you disgusting person!"

I tried to keep myself together. I was so close to crying. I had to keep on repeating to myself: It is just the Heart of Time making her say the wrong stuff. It is just the Heart of Time making her say the wrong stuff.

"Don't listen to what I say, just help me take it off."

Bella forced the words out of her mouth with a lot of trouble. The Heart of Time was so powerful. "Don't you dare ignore my commands!" she said.

I nodded and reached for the necklace. The gem was a really light shade of red, but it was red nonetheless. When I touched it, I jumped back and screamed. The Heart of Time had stung me, and it felt like I had held fire in my hands.

"I'm so sorry, Amber. You deserved that, you idiot! I didn't mean that." Bella said. The struggle she was going through was very painful. It took a while before my hand finally felt normal.

I helped Bella up by her arms. Sara came to help her up.

"What should we do?" Sara asked after I told her what the necklace did when I tried to remove it.

"I don't know. I think we should take her to The Mother of it All," I said.

Sara nodded and led the way back to The Mother of it All's headquarters.

Working hard is important, but there is something that matters even more. Believing in yourself.

Harry Potter

Chapter ELEVEN

When we finally got to The Mother of it All's place, Sara and I were on the verge of tears. Bella tried very hard to control herself, but the necklace forced her to do mean things. She pulled our hair, stepped on our feet, and made sure to insult us. It was all we could do to not break down in tears. Somehow, we kept it together and silently hoped it would be over soon.

"Well, isn't this an ugly place," Bella said snidely, taking a look around. Then she continued sarcastically, "This should be fun." Sara and I tried our best not to burst out in laughter and agreement at her foul comment.

We found Mother Nature, The Mother of it All in her chair, looking as weird as she had the first time.

"And what an ugly lady too!" Bella said, quite impolitely. For some reason, it had no effect on the old woman. It was as if she hadn't heard. Nonetheless, Sara and I tried to hush Bella.

I didn't even feel like I was in the same place that I had visited last time. The only difference between our last meeting and today was the fact that I was more confident and, instead of dreaming about what I could achieve, I had gone and achieved something. Although I couldn't take the Heart of Time off, I had been successful in helping Bella reduce the red fog. And I guess that positivity had been enough to change the whole environment of this place.

I had cleared my throat before I called The Mother of it All.

"Amber," she said, pronouncing my name as weirdly and creepily she had before. "How is everything going? Is there any improvement in our situation?"

"Wow, creepy lady alert!" Bella said rudely.

I almost gave death glares to both Bella and The Mother of it All. Did The Mother of it All not see Bella right between Sara and me?

And then it hit me. I remembered that The Mother of it All was not able to see the Heart of Time or its current owner.

"Yes, ma'am. I have Bella with us—she is the girl who is wearing the Heart of Time. You probably can't see her right now, but Sara and I are holding her," I said quickly.

"Oh!" The Mother of it All exclaimed, slapping her forehead for not realizing the obvious. "I'm sorry, dear. The Heart of Time doesn't allow me to even know of the existence of the person who is holding it. So I can't see, hear, smell, or touch them. They basically don't exist in my life. That's why I needed you."

"What a dumb old woman," Bella said. Sara and I winced and tried our best to ignore her words.

"Why didn't you take the Heart of Time from her?" The Mother of it All asked.

"That's why we came here, The Mother of it All. You see, for some reason, when I touched the necklace to take it off, it burned me," I said with a shudder. "I don't know what I can do to take it off."

"Hmm… does the gem have any red left?" The Mother of it All asked.

Sara quickly looked at the Heart of Time. Its red was slowly fading. "Not really. It's just a small fog of really, really light pink," she said, looking up again.

"That's the problem, dears," The Mother of it All

said. "Until it is empty of color—crystal clear—it will only hurt anyone who tries to take it off, and it will not let itself be taken off the person wearing it."

"So, now what?" I asked desperately.

"Now, you have to help her remove it completely," The Mother of it All replied.

"How?" I asked.

"I'm afraid I do not know, dear. The Heart of Time has many attributes, and to bring it to good, you have to perform good acts," The Mother of it All said. "What did you do that reduced the red fog?"

Sara told her the whole story. About the angry girl, about the fireballs, and about me protecting the girl.

"Hmm... sacrifice," The Mother of it All said thoughtfully. A moment of silence followed. She seemed to be thinking about what we had told her.

"What?" I asked, encouraging her.

"Why does this woman say dumb things?" Bella asked coolly. Sara and I ignored her—as we had been doing the whole time.

"You sacrificed yourself to save the other girl. No wonder. The Heart of Time will return to good upon a sacrifice. Bella was supposed to sacrifice herself for me, but something happened, and she made a mistake that triggered the red fog. When I first saw her, I was positive she was a pure blood, and she was at the time. But I guess her mistake cost us all peace. And then you sacrificed yourself trying to help her. You could've gotten hurt. You're so lucky that she resisted and the Heart of Time couldn't handle it.

"I believe that now you're going to have to do something relating to sacrifice to get rid of the small amount of fog remaining in the crystal. While you do that, you and Bella can stay inside one of the rooms in the headquarters," The Mother of it All explained.

"Hey! Old lady! I'm standing right here!" Bella shouted. "Why do you dimwits keep ignoring me?" Sara and I controlled ourselves yet again. It was so hard not to answer her.

"How long do you think it will take?" I asked.

"It depends on Bella, dear. It could be as quick as half an hour, or it could take as long as forever—which we do not have. We can't risk letting this continue. You need to hit home for her and do or say something that will touch her," The Mother of it All said.

"Okay. Thank you, Mother of it All," I said. I can do this! I thought to myself.

"You're welcome, Amber. Thank you for all if your help and sacrifice," she said as she gave us directions to the room.

As Sara and I started to lead Bella away, The Mother of it All called Sara. "Sara, I need to speak to you," The Mother of it All said. Immediately, bells started ringing in my mind. I found it really weird that The Mother of it All was holding Sara back. She never did that—well, she hadn't in the time I had known her—but then again, Sara had known The Mother of it All longer than I had. Maybe there was something unrelated that they had to discuss.

Had I not been in a hurry, I would've listened in on their conversation. As it was, the words I overheard spiked my curiosity.

"She didn't ask you anything, did she?" The Mother of it All asked. That was all I had heard before Bella started with her nonsense again.

"You've become like a crazy person, Bella," I said, shaking my head.

"I know," my Bella said, and then the Heart of Time Bella said, "Don't you dare call me crazy!"

All things are difficult before they are easy.

Thomas Fuller

Chapter TWELVE

After a few minutes, we got to the room, and I helped Bella to have a seat. I talked to her about how she used to be and what she had become. I took my time, telling her stories that I remembered but, although my Bella remembered, the Heart of Time's Bella said many bitter things. They hurt my feelings, but I let them slide.

Sacrifice, I told myself over and over again.

I didn't let it get to me, and I took blow after blow after blow of her negative attitude towards my positivity. I tried to bring a positive light to the things she said.

I knew I was struggling against time. Then I remembered that the last time the Heart of Time had faltered was when I sang a song that Bella knew.

If I let this situation drag on any longer, this place would be overflowing with ghosts. I was afraid to think of what would happen if the population of the ghosts crossed the limit.

Eventually, silence enveloped us. I didn't know what to do, so I started singing.

"Bella, listen here right now.

I am telling you this once and for all.

I want you to listen closely now.

Do you not remember the time when you helped an old lady to get across the street?

(She'd done that many times.)

Do you remember the time when you solved a bullying problem?

Do you remember the time my mom died? You

helped me feel better.

We are all in this together.

Surprisingly, Bella listened on quietly. Tears fell from my eyes.

"Bella, please help me," I pleaded. My heart was broken, and it was so hard to be strong.

Bella looked at me. The Heart of Time's shield was breaking, slowly.

"Sing," she whispered. An instant later, the other Bella came back. "Don't you dare sing with that disgusting voice!" she said.

I smiled. I had gotten the message, and I knew that Bella loved my voice.

She loved hearing me sing, and so, I sang the song that meant the world to both of us.

"There's only one person, you can trust.
She is the one inside you that you must, figure out.
It's hard to find her.
But she is inside.
She'll come when she is most,
Needed, needed
And she is going to rise from the Earth
And she is going to rise to the sky,
And she is going to teach you how to fly.
How to fly."

And at that moment, the most miraculous thing happened.

The spell broke!

Bella started crying and, by the time her second tear dropped, the Heart of Time had become crystal clear! She sang the last line with me.

I hugged Bella tightly and made sure the gem was crystal clear before taking it off.

Bella hugged me really hard. "Thank you, thank you so much, Amber! I couldn't breathe with that necklace. I wasn't me, and I'm so sorry for anything mean I said to hurt your feelings or anyone's feelings. It was so hard to control it. And when you sang—oh, when you sang!—you did it! I was fighting the power inside; I tried really hard not to let it take control, and when you sang, I felt like I could fly! And I found the girl inside that I could trust, and I fought the Heart of Time. Thank you so much!"

"I missed you so much, Bella!" I yelled happily.

"I missed you too!" Bella cried with the same excitement.

And with that, we ran to Sara and The Mother of it All, who were having a very interesting conversation with lots of gestures.

I ignored this and ran in with the necklace in my hand. "We did it!" I yelled.

"Oh my God!" Sara looked horrified while The Mother of it All looked at me with guilt.

"What happened? We did it; that's it! We get to rest in peace and go to the afterlife. Finally!" I said joyfully. Dreams and future expectations started forming in my mind. We would get through this.

But Sara and The Mother of it All ignored me as they looked at each other.

Bella stood beside me. "What is going on?" She asked me in a whisper.

"I don't know," I whispered back. My heart began to sink. Suddenly, it felt like this wasn't the end after all.

"I'm afraid we are not done yet," The Mother of it All said.

I wasn't ready for what I had to hear next.

If you don't stay together through the bad, then you won't be together for the good.

Cecily Morgan

Chapter THIRTEEN

"What do you mean?" Bella asked.

"What are you talking about?" I asked at the same time. I was worried and, moreover, angry. I had gone through so much, and here she was, the person who started all of this, saying I wasn't done yet! The irony!

"Remember when I told you that the Heart of Time needs to be worn by someone with a pure heart who sacrifices himself or herself for the rest of the world? We need someone to sacrifice their afterlife for everyone else and wear the Heart of Time here, in the in-between world. The same way I did," The Mother of it All said slowly as Sara nodded along.

"You knew about this?" I asked her.

She looked down guilty. "Yes. I'm sorry."

I stared at her for a bit and was surprised at how naïve we are sometimes, that we take people for exactly who they seem to be.

"And you guys have chosen me to do this?"

They both nodded.

"We don't have time. Someone has to wear it as soon as possible before the ghosts start deteriorating. Even I don't know where they go after that. Slowly, they will lose shape and form and literally become nothing and disappear. I've seen a few deteriorate when I became The Mother of it All. We have fifteen minutes from the time that it was removed from Bella to find a Sacrificer. And we need a pure heart, Amber. Please."

I looked at them like they were crazy. They were asking me to give up my whole afterlife for everyone and, even though I understood where they were coming from, I couldn't believe that they had hidden the truth from me.

"How can you expect me to decide whether or not I want to sacrifice my afterlife in, like, the next fifteen minutes?"

"I know, dear, but think of the betterment of everyone else," The Mother of it All said as she walked toward me and took the Heart of Time from my hand.

"No!" Bella screamed. "Amber, listen, I can't let you go through what I had to suffer from. Please, trust me. Leave it to someone else."

The Mother of it All ignored her as she unclasped the hook of the necklace.

"Do I even have a choice?" I asked.

"I'm afraid not," she said with a shrug as she put it around my neck. "I'm sorry, Amber. I need you to wear the Heart of Time." Right before she clasped the hook, she looked at me. "Are your intentions pure, dear? I wouldn't want a repeat of what we had before."

"Hold on," I said.

The Mother of it All stopped.

"When you close it, everyone leaves?"

"Everyone, yes."

"Is there a way for me to stay with her?" Bella asked.

"What?!" I exclaimed. "No. Bella, you need to go."

"No," Bella said stubbornly. Then she looked at The Mother of it All. "Is there a way?"

"Yes," she said and, suddenly, my heart felt like a burden had been released from it.

"What is it?" Bella asked impatiently.

"You both have to share the necklace. You will sit together and hold the in-between life. Maybe one day, you can figure out how to take turns traveling from the afterlife and this in-between life."

"Let's do it!" Bella said.

"What are you doing?" I asked.

"I'm not leaving you alone. If we're going to sacrifice ourselves for others, we're going to sacrifice ourselves together. For humanity." Bella said.

"For humanity," I repeated.

The Mother of it All did something with her hands, and suddenly a second necklace string was attached to the Heart of Time. She whispered some strange words in an unfamiliar language. Suddenly, when she pulled the strings apart, the Heart of Time came apart. Suddenly, there were two Hearts of Time. She clasped one around each of our necks.

"You both have the ability to use the power of the Heart of Time to make a world for yourselves. You get to paint your life," said The Mother of it All with a gleam in her eyes.

Bella and I held hands tightly, afraid that this might take us somewhere else and far away from each other.

The second that The Mother of it All's task was done, she and Sara slowly began to disappear. Their bodies sparkled and shimmered as a swirl of something that I would call magic went around them and took them, as dust, up to the sky.

With that, the headquarters also disappeared. Bella and I watched it go. And then all the other ghosts vanished.

"God, this is so amazing," Bella said. We watched in wonder as a sea of sparkles swirled around each of the millions of ghosts before unanimously ascending.

And with that, the world became empty. It was like living in eternal white emptiness.

There was nothing.

Bella and I laughed as each of us started thinking of things to paint our life with.

"I want gardens," I said immediately, literally jumping in delight.

"I want cats!" Bella said, one finger pointed up in the air.

"I want flowers," I said, clasping my hands together.

"I want a beach," Bella said, snapping her fingers.

And with each of our demands, the world created itself.

Neither of us knew for how long we could sacrifice ourselves, but we would spend as long as we could as we created our own paradise together.

And one day, I would go and visit Mom in Heaven. She was lucky that she didn't have to wait so restlessly with the other ghosts.

But we learned one thing that I want the humans back in Life to know: things that happen with negative intentions lead to more bad things, while things are done with a pure heart always result in good things.

THE END!

Acknowledgements

This book would never have been completed if it weren't for the following people:

First, my parents, Shahnaz Siddiqui and Ayaz Siddiqui (a.k.a., Mama and Baba), who supported me throughout my journey towards a lifetime of success and who took me out of la-la land whenever I would visit there.

My elder sisters, Sadaf Ayaz (a.k.a., Api) and Huda Ayaz, who both did whatever it took to motivate me and spent hours editing my book several times. They taught me never to give up until you finish what you have started.

My elder brother, Zaid Ayaz, and my younger sister, Marwa Ayaz, who both humored me and inspired me.

Also, my grandparents, Fateh M. Chohan, Akbary B. Chohan, Hamida Bibi, and Allah Dittah:

My paternal grandfather, Fateh M. Chohan, who always asked me the same question: "When will your book come out?" I'd always reply, "It's already out."

My dear paternal, deceased grandmother, Akbary B. Chohan, who was a big part in my writing this book and without whom I wouldn't be, and neither would this book.

My lovely maternal grandmother, Hamida Bibi, who motivated me to write my book.

And last but not least, my maternal grandfather, Allah Dittah, who has always been in my heart and who started my engine whenever it stopped working.

If I have forgotten anyone, please know that you are in my heart no matter what.

About the author

Maliha Ayaz is an 11 year old author who chose the path of writing to full fill her duty towards her favorite sport, talking. Writing was the only way she found a bit more joy of doing it. With the help of the books she has read and the help of her love for words and day dreaming, she may have just found that little something that her destiny has told her to do. She started writing when she was in second grade and has always wished and continues to write as a fifth grader.